WOODPECKER
Wants a Waffle

Written and illustrated by **Steve Breen**

HARPER
An Imprint of HarperCollinsPublishers

To Matthew

Woodpecker Wants a Waffle
Copyright © 2016 by Steve Breen
All rights reserved. Manufactured in China. No part of this book
may be used or reproduced in any manner whatsoever without
written permission except in the case of brief quotations embodied in critical
articles and reviews. For information address HarperCollins Children's Books,
a division of HarperCollins Publishers, 195 Broadway, New York, NY 10007.
www.harpercollinschildrens.com

Library of Congress Cataloging-in-Publication Data
Breen, Steve, author, illustrator.
  Woodpecker wants a waffle / by Steve Breen. — First edition.
   pages cm
  Summary: "Benny the woodpecker makes a brilliant plan to eat a tasty plate of
waffles"— Provided by publisher.
  ISBN 978-0-06-234257-7 (hardcover)
  [1. Determination (Personality trait)—Fiction. 2. Woodpeckers—Fiction.
3. Pancakes, waffles, etc.—Fiction. 4. Animals—Fiction. 5. Food habits—Fiction.]
  I. Title.
PZ7.B748228Woo 2016   2014041209
[E]—dc23   CIP
                                                                      AC

The artist used his artistic genius, waterproof black ink, watercolors,
and colored pencils to create the illustrations in this book.
Typography by Rachel Zegar
16 17 18 19 20   SCP   10 9 8 7 6 5 4 3 2 1
❖
First Edition

One morning, Benny awoke to the best tummy-rumbling smell.

So off he flew to investigate.

"W-A-F-F-L-E," he read. "What in the world is a waffle?"

The waffles smelled good.
The waffles looked good.
The waffles must taste good too, thought Benny.

"I want waffles," Benny declared.

Benny politely pecked on the front door.

But instead of waffles, he got the BOOT.

Next he tried to sneak in. . . .

But instead of waffles, Benny got swept away.

Benny tried a number of creative disguises . . .

but instead of waffles, he was TOSSED in the trash.

SWOOSH!

"What are you doing?" asked Bunny.
"I am wishing for waffles," said Benny.

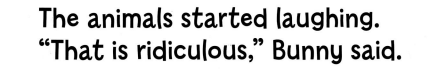

The animals started laughing.
"That is ridiculous," Bunny said.

One by one, the other animals chimed in.

"Well, why not?" Benny asked.

"Why not?" the animals grumbled,
chirped, croaked, and whispered.

They thought, and thought, and
thought, and thought. . . .

"Because I SAID so," said Bunny.

"I really don't have time for this 'said so' nonsense," Benny said impatiently.

Benny got right to work devising a plan to get some waffles....

FOOM!

"First, I will shoot out of a cannon,

then moonwalk

and break-dance,

followed by a stand-up comedy act with

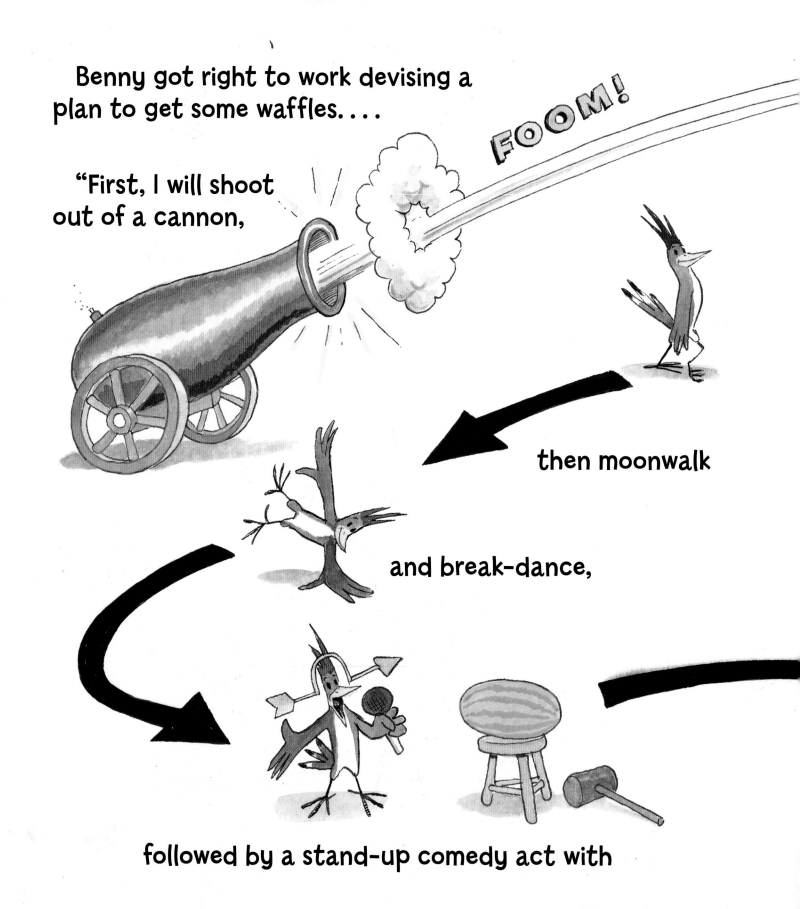

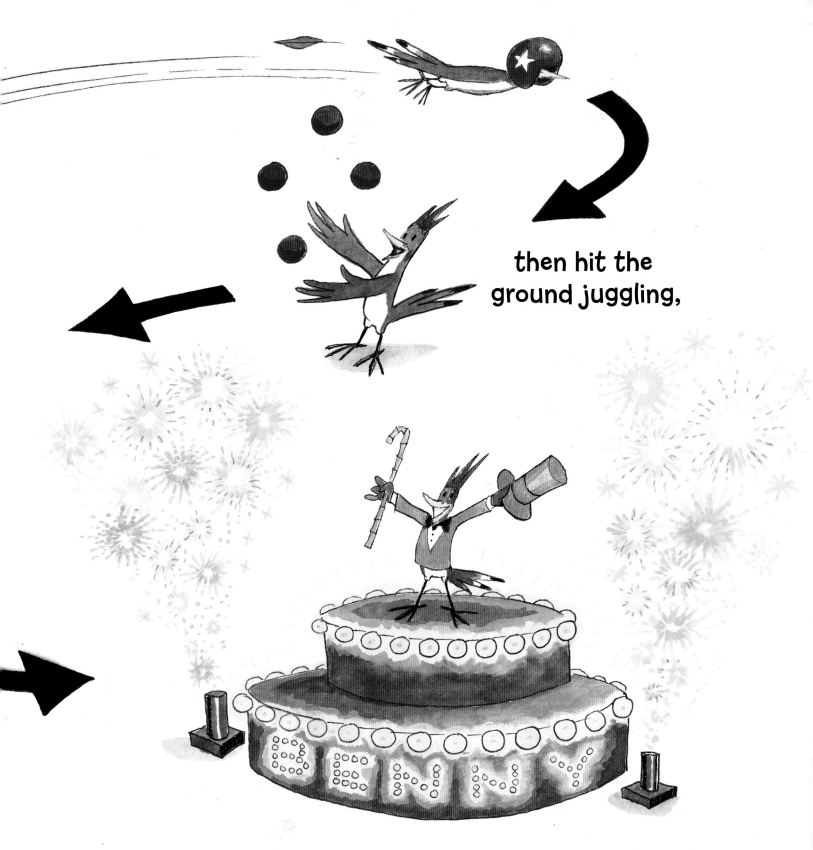

then hit the
ground juggling,

a Broadway-style finale featuring fireworks."

The animals were speechless,
though Benny was sure he heard
some snickering.

"See you all tomorrow!
Don't be late!"

The next morning, the animals gathered in the field by the diner to catch Benny's big show. No one was late.
No one except Benny.

As the animals waited patiently for Benny to arrive, the waitress in the diner noticed something odd. The customers noticed something strange too.

Everyone at the diner stepped outside to look at the animals.

That's when Benny made his move.

"Sweet," said Benny.